MONSTER ✷ HIGH
Welcome to Boo York

Adapted by **Perdita Finn**

Based on the screenplay
by **Keith Wagner**

LITTLE, BROWN & COMPANY
LB kids

Copyright © 2015 Mattel, Inc. All rights reserved. MONSTER HIGH and associated trademarks
are owned by and used under license from Mattel, Inc.

Little, Brown and Company

Hachette Book Group
1290 Avenue of the Americas, New York, NY 10104
Visit us at lb-kids.com

LB kids is an imprint of Little, Brown and Company.
The LB kids name and logo are trademarks of Hachette Book Group, Inc.

The publisher is not responsible for websites (or their content) that are not owned by the publisher.

First Edition: September 2015

Library of Congress Control Number: 2015944669

ISBN 978-0-316-30115-2

10 9 8 7 6 5 4 3 2 1

CW

Printed in the United States of America

Catty Noir had been the purrfect princess of pop—but she left the spotlight for the halls of Monster High. "I have to find my own voice, my own music," she whispered to herself at her keyboard.

But would it ever happen? Would she ever know what love really was? Would she ever sing onstage again?

In the Creepateria, Cleo de Nile had **clawesome news**: She was headed to Boo York for the comet gala!

"I'm so excited, I'm about to burst through my bandages," exclaimed Cleo.

"I hear that in Boo York they play music on every street corner," Operetta said with a sigh.

Cleo grinned. "My dad did say I could bring a friend. Or two...or...**ALL OF YOU!**"

Operetta, Frankie Stein, Draculaura, and Clawdeen Wolf cheered. It was time to pack.

Catty was excited too. Maybe she would find her voice in Boo York.

The ghouls got out of the subway at the Forty-Second Screech station. They wanted to check out the fashions at the boo-tiques and get their gowns for the gala.

Everyone was excited about the once-in-thirteen-hundred-years comet that would pass over the city at midnight. There was going to be a big party at the Museum of Unnatural History.

Catty wasn't the only ghoul looking for her voice in Boo York. Luna Mothews was a Boo Jersey ghoul who **loved to perform** more than anything else. She was lured to Boo York by the bright lights of Bloodway.

Elle Eedee was a robot DJ spinning discs on the street.

"Voltageously electric!" squealed Frankie.

"You ghouls must be here for the Ptolemys' gala. That comet must be pretty **special**. I'm gonna DJ!"

Back at Monster High, an alarm buzzed on Ghoulia Yelps's iCoffin. She raced down to her laboratory to find out what was wrong. An image of the comet appeared on the computer screen. Ghoulia gasped. The comet wasn't going to pass over Boo York—it was going to crash into it!

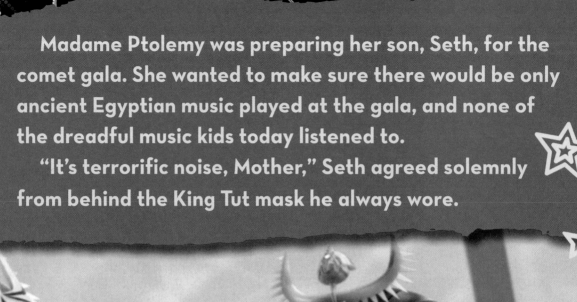

Madame Ptolemy was preparing her son, Seth, for the comet gala. She wanted to make sure there would be only ancient Egyptian music played at the gala, and none of the dreadful music kids today listened to.

"It's terrorific noise, Mother," Seth agreed solemnly from behind the King Tut mask he always wore.

Abbey Bominable, the daughter of the Yeti, peeked over Ghoulia's shoulder. What was happening? Why was the comet headed right toward Boo York?

Both ghouls looked at the screen. There had to be a way to stop the comet. Could they do it **before midnight**? Ghoulia's hands flew across the keyboard as she tried to come up with a plan.

The ghouls were headed to the Monster of Liberty when they saw a street rapper wowing the crowd. His eyes lit up when he saw Catty. *"Everybody calls me by my old name. Ugh, so lame. You can just call me Pharaoh."*

"Be the **star of the show** *when you are out in Boo York,"* Catty answered him in song.

The crowd went wild. They recognized the princess of pop. Catty and Pharaoh raced up a fire escape to flee the crowd.

"Hi! I'm Catty Noir!" said Catty, catching her breath.

"I know." Pharaoh laughed. "We sounded pretty good together."

Heath Burns and Manny Taur saw Ghoulia and Abbey staring at the computer and pressing buttons. What a cool new game!

Heath pushed the ghouls aside and took over the controls. He was trying to crash a satellite into the comet, but the comet was sending out a protective force field.

Ghoulia groaned. Comets didn't do that.

Maybe the comet wasn't a comet at all. Maybe it was a...

"Spaceship!" cried Abbey.

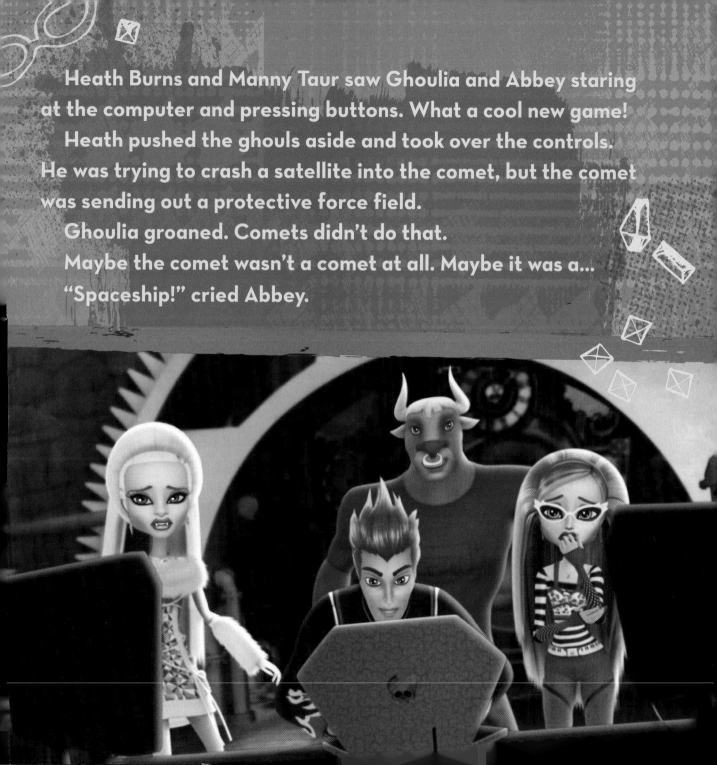

Pharaoh took Catty to the top of the Monster of Liberty. They could see the whole city—and hear it too. At first, it sounded like noise to Catty, but when she shut her eyes, she could hear the rhythm of the traffic, the beat of the voices, and the songs of the city. "I hear music!" exclaimed Catty. "I've found my music!"

She opened her eyes, and Pharaoh was smiling at her.

Once Abbey and Ghoulia realized the comet was a spaceship, all they had to do to save the world was contact the pilot. But how could they do that? Would the pilot listen to them? Was the pilot even awake? Those were the questions, but Ghoulia didn't know the answers...yet.

The ghouls had no idea how much **danger** they
were in. They were getting ready for the comet
gala. Operetta helped Draculaura with her makeup
because vampires can't see themselves in mirrors.
Once they were all dressed, the ghouls strutted
around their hotel room like it was a runway show.

Catty wanted to know how Pharaoh had become a rapper. "I don't know how to tell you this, but...I'm a mummy!" Pharaoh admitted to Catty that he was going to stop performing because his family didn't like his music.

Catty couldn't believe it. "I stopped singing because I wasn't being true to myself. But you, you sing from your heart. You've found your voice. Why would you give that up?"

"It's complicated" was all Pharaoh would say before they parted.

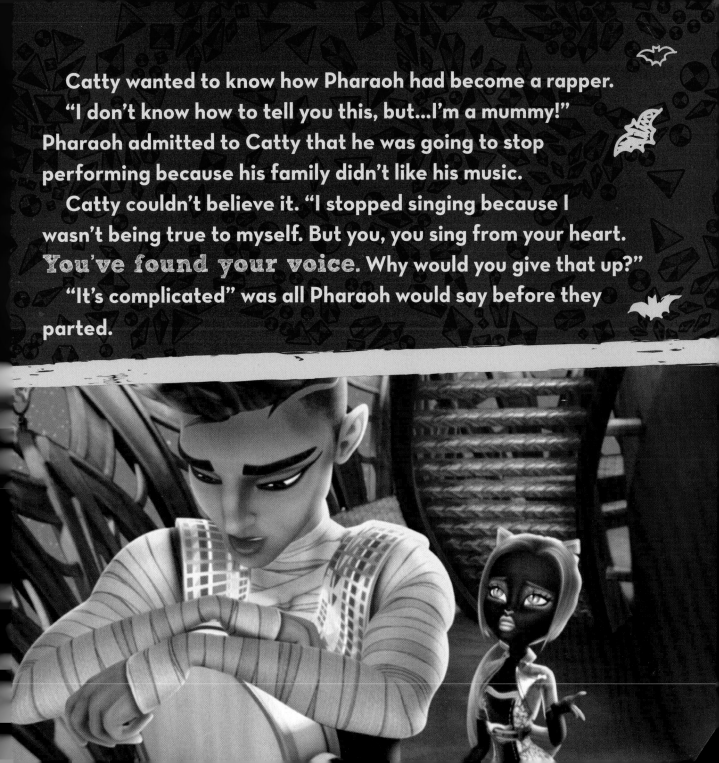

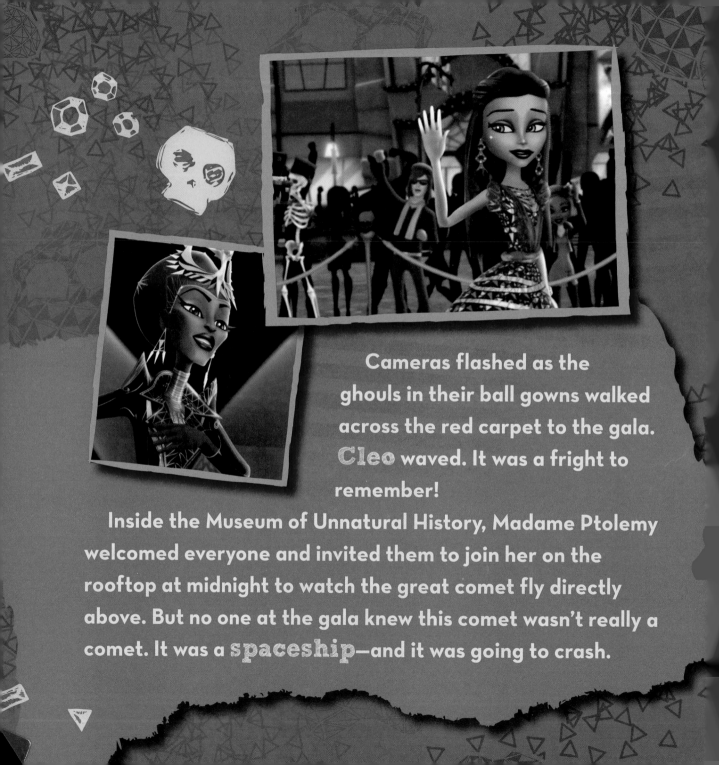

Cameras flashed as the ghouls in their ball gowns walked across the red carpet to the gala. Cleo waved. It was a fright to remember!

Inside the Museum of Unnatural History, Madame Ptolemy welcomed everyone and invited them to join her on the rooftop at midnight to watch the great comet fly directly above. But no one at the gala knew this comet wasn't really a comet. It was a spaceship—and it was going to crash.

Just after Madame Ptolemy made her announcement, Seth pulled off his mask. "I'm not going to let you take my voice away," he told his mother.

Catty whirled around. She couldn't believe it. She knew that voice. It was Pharaoh. Seth *was* Pharaoh!

"I have found my voice!" he told the crowd. He began rapping, and Catty began singing with him.

The prince of Boo York was the king of the streets!

The ghouls were happy for Catty, but something was wrong with Elle Eedee. The robot DJ was fritzing out. She buzzed and pulsed. The museum filled with earsplitting feedback. Elle Eedee was in a trance. She seemed to have lost her ability to create music. Did it have something to do with the comet?

Ghoulia was charting data on a blackboard. Things weren't looking good for Boo York—or the comet. The mansters were still playing with the satellites on the computer.

Manny pumped his fist in the air. "Triple score!" He strummed an invisible air guitar in celebration.

Ghoulia whirled around. But then it hit her. Maybe all of this had something to do with music. But what?

Ghoulia's iCoffin buzzed. Frankie was calling about Elle. She held the phone up so Ghoulia could hear the strange noises their new ghoulfriend was making.

Ghoulia realized the strange electronic sounds coming through the phone were music notes. They were the same notes coming from the comet. She took out a keyboard and began to play. That was how she would reach the pilot—with **music from the satellites**!

Seeing how happy Pharaoh was with Catty, Madame Ptolemy forgave her son. Everyone went up to the rooftop to celebrate. But that's when they saw that the comet was coming closer and closer, heading right toward Boo York!

Cleo's sister, Nefera, pointed up at the sky. Draculaura screamed. "The comet. It's coming right for us!"

But Catty wasn't terrified—she was listening to the music coming from the satellites, thanks to Ghoulia. It was a **beautiful melody**, and Catty couldn't resist it. She began singing along. Hearing her voice, Pharaoh harmonized with her. Guests stopped and stared at them. Draculaura and Clawdeen began singing too. Then Deuce and Cleo lifted their voices as well.

What no one knew was that the music had **awakened** the being inside the comet. She was at the controls at last!

There was a giant flash, the comet exploded into shimmering dots of light, and a glowing orb hovered over the rooftop. Out of it stepped a star creature!

"My name is Astranova. That song you heard was a distress signal—**you all saved me!**"

Catty was also grateful. "You were the one who saved us! If your comet hadn't brought us all here, Pharaoh and I wouldn't have found our voices. **Welcome to Boo York!**"

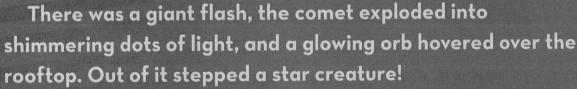

Everyone on the roof began singing with Astranova, the glamorous star girl.

"*We are shooting stars, light it up, be who you are! Burn in the sky, hear the sound of our voice, make the world recognize us. Hear the sound of the crowd, celebration of who we are. We are here to light up the night! We are shooting stars! Be who you are!*"